Find out what happens when the Playschool Babies make a story about a witch into a special pantomime . . .

My Little Pony

PLAYSCHOOL PANTOMIME

written by Pat Posner
illustrated by
David Clark Design Group Ltd.

Copyright © 1991 Hasbro Inc.
All rights reserved.
Published in Great Britain by World International Publishing Limited,
an Egmont Company, Egmont House, PO Box 111, Great Ducie Street,
Manchester M60 3BL.
Printed in Germany.
ISBN 0 7498 0425 4

A CIP catalogue record for this book is available from the British Library

Lady Lessons is a *very* clever pony. The
Playschool Babies love their teacher . . .
her lessons are such good fun!

One Friday afternoon, she reached
into her desk and pulled out a story book.
"Are you all listening?" she asked.

"Yes, Lady Lessons!" replied the Playschool Babies.

"That's good!" laughed Lady Lessons. "But I am not going to tell you a story. You are going to tell me one."

"But we can't read properly!" said Baby Alphabet.

"We could look at the pictures in the book and make the words up!" said Baby Pictures.

"Well done, Baby Pictures!" said Lady Lessons. "Come up to my desk and get the book."

The first picture was of a witch. The witch was stirring something in a big pan.

"The witch is making a magic spell!" said Baby Pictures. "Baby Count-a-Lot, *you* pretend to be the witch."

"I wish I had a spoon and a big pan,"
sighed Baby Count-a-Lot.

"A witch's pan is called a cauldron,"
Lady Lessons told the babies.

"I wish I had a spoon and a cauldron!"
said Baby Count-a-Lot.

Lady Lessons reached into the classroom cupboard and pulled out . . .

Yes! She pulled out a cauldron.

"Happy hooves! Thank you!" said the baby pony. "Now I can pretend to be the witch in the story."

"Wait a shake of a mane!" said Baby Pictures. "You need a spoon."

"I'll find a spoon!" said Baby Alphabet. "I'll look in the alphabet drawers. S is for spoon."

"You need something to stir with the spoon!" said Baby Schoolbag. "I think I've got a bottle of lemonade in my schoolbag."

Baby Schoolbag clicked his back hooves together, and all sorts of things piled up in front of him. But there wasn't a bottle of lemonade!

"I'll put the acorns and this toy frog in the cauldron!" laughed Baby Count-a-Lot.

Baby Alphabet found a wooden spoon with a long handle. She gave it to Baby Count-a-Lot.

"Now we can start the story!" said Baby Pictures. "One day, Cranky Witch was very busy. She was stirring up a special mixture in her cauldron."

Baby Pictures turned to the next picture in the book. "Oh!" she said. "Cranky Witch poured the mixture into a bottle."

"We haven't got a bottle!" said Baby Schoolbag.

Baby Pictures found a piece of paper and drew a picture of a bottle.

"Happy hooves!" said Baby Count-a-Lot. "I've got an idea! We don't need the story book to tell Lady Lessons a story. We can make up a story of our own!"

Lady Lessons smiled. "You can turn the story into a pantomime!"

"We must have a princess in our pantomime!" said Baby Alphabet. "I'll find a crown."

"I'll help you!" said Baby Schoolbag. "Oh, look. I've found a clown suit and a clock. We can use these in our pantomime, too!"

"I've found some curtains!" said Baby Alphabet. "We can make a stage. I'll ask Lady Lessons to hang the curtains up in front of our desks."

Of course, Lady Lessons found a curtain pole in the cupboard!

"I'll draw a picture of a gloomy palace n some gloomy woods," decided Baby Pictures. "The princess lives there and she's very unhappy."

"I'll practise looking sad," said Baby Alphabet.

"I can use my abacus in the pantomime!" said Baby Count-a-Lot, happily. "We can pretend the clock is striking and I'll count how many times it strikes. Cranky Witch is a good witch. At four o'clock she's going to the gloomy palace with a laughing spell!"

"I'll be a clown!" said Baby Schoolbag. "I jump out of your spell bottle, Cranky Witch, and make the sad princess laugh."

"I'll draw a picture of a piano," said Baby Pictures. "I'll pretend to play happy music when the princess laughs!"

Before long, everything was ready.
The Playschool Babies called to Lady
Lessons. "The pantomime is about to
start!" they said.

Cranky Witch started to stir the mixture
in her cauldron . . . Baby Pictures started
to open the curtains. Then . . .

"Come and peep through the curtains!" she whispered to the other Playschool Babies. "You're going to get a *very* big surprise when you see who's there!"

Lady Lessons had invited the Schooltime Ponies to the pantomime!

"I hope we can remember what we're supposed to do," thought Baby Pictures, as she pulled the curtains open.

"Welcome to our pantomime," she said. "Cranky Witch is stirring up a magic mixture."

"Heavy hooves! I've forgotten to put the acorns and the frog into the cauldron. I haven't got anything to stir!" wailed Baby Count-a-Lot.

Sports-time kicked his heels three times. "How's this?" he snorted – and five ping-pong balls bounced into the cauldron!

The pantomime continued. When anything went wrong, one of the Schooltime Ponies came to the rescue! Baby Alphabet kept laughing when she *should* have looked sad!

Painting-time used her special face paints to give the Playschool Baby a sad face!

When the clown appeared to make the
sad princess laugh, Play-time wiggled
her nose and a skipping rope landed next
to Baby Schoolbag.

"Heavy hooves! I'm no good at
skipping!" said Baby Schoolbag. He
made *all* the ponies laugh!

"Because the sad princess was happy, everything in the gloomy palace was happy, too!" Baby Pictures told the audience. "And if you listen carefully, you will hear some happy music!"

Music-time chuckled and blinked her eyes!

Suddenly, all the musical instruments jumped out of the music cupboard and played by themselves. All except the triangle . . . Music-time played that!

It was a lovely ending to the pantomime. Wasn't Lady Lessons clever when she invited the Schooltime Ponies to watch?